Willie
The Moose Who Saved Christmas

By
Michael MacCurtain

Printed in Korea

National Library of Canada Cataloguing in Publication Data

A cataloguing record for this book that includes the U.S. Library of Congress Classification number, the Library of Congress Call number and the Dewey Decimal cataloguing code is available from the National Library of Canada. The complete cataloguing record can be obtained from the National Library's online database at: www.nlc-bnc.ca/amicus/index-e.html

ISBN 1-4120-1932-X

For:

Matt, Mike and Kate
For all the Christmas
smiles they have given me

This is a story, a Christmas tale
of Willie the Moose and his strange travail
'Twas through the north woods on Christmas Eve he did trek
When he stumbled upon a very strange wreck
There in the woods the driver lay dazed
As on reindeer and presents our Willie gazed!

So sniffing and snorting the fat man's beard he did lick,
And in this gross fashion he awakened Saint Nick.

Santa gave a holler, a scream and a shout
As he hit his head on Willie's wet snout!
Then standing and looking, the damage he saw
Took the red from his cheeks and the pipe from his jaw.
His reindeer lay injured, unable to fly.
His sleigh was grounded; no more for the sky.

As this problem he pondered, Santa had no doubt
That Christmas this year was to be a washout
No candy, no presents, no kids shouts of joy
For on Christmas morning there'd not be a toy
Under tree nor in stockings, these homes would be sad,
And the thought of this horror made Santa quite mad!

So gathering the harness and stretching it loose,
He fitted it on Willie, his new Christmas moose.
Then taking the light from Rudolph's nose of red
He placed it on the antlers atop Willie's head.

Then one crack of the whip, as Santa well knew,
And into the air our brave Willie flew!
Up like a bird toward the stars he did head
Pulling behind him Saint Nick and his sled

Turning left, turning right, with his antlers a blinking,
He headed for Portland and was there in a twinkling.

Now it wasn't the clatter of reindeer you heard on your roof;
'Twas the clippity clop of the Christmas moose hoofs!

From Portland to Boston, from New York to Philly,
Christmas came from the sky on a sleigh pulled by Willie.
From Atlanta to Greenville to old Tennessee,
Willie made sure that Christmas brought glee.
Over the heartland folks heard Santa Cry
"On Willie! On Willie!" and Willie's snort in reply!

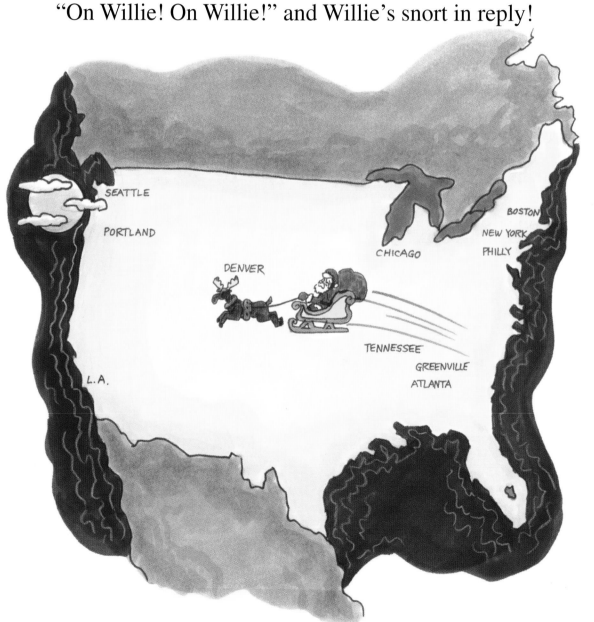

In Chicago and Denver pilots reported the sight
Of a sleigh and a moose flying into the night!

In L.A. and Seattle and Vancouver B.C.,
Willie saved Christmas for you and for me.

As the sun rose in the East and the Moon set in the West
In the great north woods our team stopped for a rest
Then Santa sent Willie back to his home;
No more on Christmas will our Willie roam
O'er mountain or roof top, o'er ocean or lake,
Just to save Christmas for all children's sake.

Still they say there's a smile on one animal Santa set loose,
It's the smile of Willie the bold Christmas moose!